Anonymous

Percy's year of rhymes

Anonymous

Percy's year of rhymes

ISBN/EAN: 9783337259488

Printed in Europe, USA, Canada, Australia, Japan

Cover: Foto ©Andreas Hilbeck / pixelio.de

More available books at **www.hansebooks.com**

PERCY'S

YEAR OF RHYMES

𝕽𝖎𝖛𝖊𝖗𝖘𝖎𝖉𝖊 𝕻𝖗𝖊𝖘𝖘·

PUBLISHED BY HURD AND HOUGHTON

459 BROOME STREET, NEW YORK

1867

RIVERSIDE, CAMBRIDGE:
STEREOTYPED AND PRINTED BY
H. O. HOUGHTON AND COMPANY.

CONTENTS.

MOTHER GOOSE'S PARTY. P. 5.

PERCY'S YEAR OF RHYMES.

MOTHER GOOSE'S PARTY.

OOD Mother Goose was growing old,
Her stories, too, were nearly told,
Her enemies were growing stronger,
She thought she should n't live much
   longer;
And ere she went for good and all,
She said she 'd give a parting ball.
So, on her wondrous broomstick car,
On which she rode so high and far,
She started to invite her guests,
And give them all her last behests.

She asked her friends and children all,
From Humpty Dumpty on the wall
To the great giant Fee-Faw-Fum,
And every body said he 'd come.

The night arrived, and Mother Goose
Had swept and garnished all her house,
Wound up the clock where the little mouse stayed,
And then herself in her best arrayed;
And while she waits her earliest guest
I 'll tell how Mother Goose was drest.

She wore her cap with stiff high crown;
Of yellow velvet was her gown;
Her stomacher of finest lace,
Lit by a sparkling diamond's blaze;
Big silver buckles on each shoe;
O'er all, a cloak of scarlet hue:
Old Mother Goose was thus drest out,
Although, in truth, there is no doubt
That while her dress had once been rare,
It now looked somewhat worse for wear.

And now through the oft-opened door
The crowd of guests began to pour:
First, the Old Woman from the shoe,
With all her children — not a few —
She came thus early, so she said,
To get the children back to bed;

Mother Goose's Party.

Next Humpty Dumpty waddled in,
All muffled up from foot to chin;
Soon after her came Cinderella,
Followed by Jack, the Giant-killer.

Little Bopeep looked very fine,
She came with brave young Valentine;
While Orson followed in their train,
Though that he could not dance was plain.
Jack Spratt and wife came in together;
She talked about the melting weather,
And fanned herself — while *he* looked blue,
And said there'd be a frost, he knew.
Last Jack and Gill, quite fresh and hearty,
Came in, the latest at the party.

And now began the famous rout:
Each dancer led his partner out,
While those who could not dance at all
Looked on from seats against the wall.
First on the floor was young Jack Horner,
He led Miss Muffet from the corner;
Little Boy Blue, so kind and good,
Stepped forth with sweet Red Riding-hood.

Then Mother Goose, the dear old soul,
Made up the set with old King Cole.

The man reputed wondrous wise,
Who in the briers scratched out his eyes,
Led out the modest Daffy-down Dilly,
Who looked as fair as any lily;
Their *vis-à-vis* was famous Jack, —
Not he who giants' pates did crack,
But Jack who climbed the bean-stalk high
To seek his fortune in the sky, —
He danced with little Silver Hair,
Who shone the fairest 'mid the fair.

But if I had no lack of time,
I could n't mention in this rhyme
One half the people, great and small,
Who danced at Mother Goose's ball.
I 'll only add that Robin Hood
Had left this night his native wood,
And brought his men all drest in green,
To dance one set with Fairy Queen;
And that all said the belle of the feast
Was sweet young Beauty with the Beast.

There was no stop to all the fun
Till dance was o'er and supper done;
Then Mother Goose, with quaking voice,
Which scarce was heard above the noise,
Informed her guests she wished to say
One word before they went away.
All listened then, with open ears,
For they revered her many years,
Besides, her counsel and advice
Her friends esteemed beyond all price.

"My dears," the good old dame began,
"Of late, 't is said in books of man,
That we are naughty useless creatures,
Who have no real forms or features;
That oft the mind of tender youth
Is poisoned by our sad untruth;
Indeed, I 've heard, it has been said,
Mother Goose's rhymes should not be read.
So much indeed we seem to grieve them,
I think we 'd better go and leave them.

"The race of man has turned our foes;
In fact, the world ungrateful grows;

Time was when babes, just learned to prattle,
Would throw away their bells and rattle
And cry to hear my oft-told lays;
But this was all in bygone days.
Now they are tired of me and you,
And only ask for stories true;
So, since I can no more amuse,
This night is the last of Mother Goose."

Here all turned pale, and tears were seen
To dim the eyes of Fairy Queen;
Little Boy Blue burst out a sobbing,
And all hearts felt a painful throbbing.
When lo! a patter of little feet
Is heard along the stony street, —
Patter, patter, on they come,
They mount the steps, they're in the room,
The fairest, merriest childish band
That ever was seen in all the land.

There Percy came with sparkling face,
And Charley, full of boyish grace;
Sweet Mary, gentle, kind, and fair,
Led little Dan with golden hair;

Jenny, Kate, and handsome Harry;
Freddy following sister Carry;
Witty Laura and sober Will,
Quiet Alice, with roguish Phil,
While toddling babies made up the troop, —
Never was seen so lovely a group.

Soon as the children all were there
They marched straight up to the grandame's chair,
And with their little army tried
To hem her in on every side.
Some hid beneath her cloak of scarlet,
Some pulled her gown; one saucy varlet
Perched on her back and held her cap;
A dozen climbed upon her lap;
And all, with tears and cries, declared
Old Mother Goose could not be spared.

When this she saw, one tear rolled down
The cheek all withered, wrinkled, and brown,
And as the children hugged and kissed her,
She said she 'd do whate'er they wished her.
For if the children's hearts she owned,
She cared not though the critics frowned.

'T was late when they broke up that night;
The guests went home in great delight,
And fairy folk and children all
Remembered long that famous ball.

JACK FROST.

THE winter's night was very cold,
    The very worst of weathers;
The chickens shivered in their pen
    In spite of all their feathers.
And boys and girls tucked up in bed,
    With mothers dear to love them,
Could feel how bitter cold it was
    Through blankets piled above them.

Just such a freezing night as this
    Jack Frost chose for a visit —
If you had seen the queer old boy,
    You would have cried, " Who is it ? "
His face was sharp and very thin,
    His body was no wider,

JACK FROST. P. 12.

His arms and legs were long and slim,
  Much like a long-legged spider.

His nose looked like an icicle;
  His feet, like Cinderella's,
Were shod with glass; his coat was thick,
  And white as any miller's.
He had a beard that touched his toes,
  Like the sweet fairy's brother;
In one hand fast he held a brush,
  Some pincers in the other.

And thus he glided in the room
  Where little Ned was sleeping,
And as he saw, above the clothes,
  Where Neddy's nose was peeping,
He gave it just one little tweak;
  Then turning to the casement,
He said, " I 'll paint the window-panes
  For little Ned's amazement."

Then waving round his tiny brush,
  Like stick or wand of fairy,
He worked right briskly at the glass

With touches light and airy ;
And straight the prettiest pictures rose
  ·Like places in a story,
With gardens, flowers, and palaces,
  And trees with branches hoary.

Upon one pane was huge Blue-beard,
  Whose wives forgot their duty;
And on the next, the palace high
  Where slept the enchanted beauty.
Near by, the forest thick and dark
  Where robin red-breasts hovered
Above the babies in the wood,
  Whom they with leaves had covered.

There grew the wondrous bean-stalk tall
  Where little Jack was climbing ;
If I should tell you half was there
  I ne'er should end my rhyming.
And everywhere the silver grass
  With sparkling flowers was sprinkled ;
While overhead on all the panes,
  The stars by hundreds twinkled.

GRANDMAMMA MOON. P 15.

How Neddy stared when he awoke
  To see this panorama;
He rubbed his eyes to see aright,
  Then called papa and mamma.
Papa was dreaming hard of stocks,
  Mamma of silks and laces,
And ere they woke the sun had left
  Only some watery traces.

GRANDMAMMA MOON.

GRANDMAMMA MOON sits up in the sky,
You scarce can see her she's so high;
  There she sits in her easy-chair,
On her white apron folding her hands,
And looking abroad o'er sea and lands,
  With her face so round and fair.

When the sun has traveled many a mile
And wishes to sleep and rest awhile,
  She says, " Pray go to bed,
And sleep quite sound while watch I keep;

No harm shall happen when you 're asleep,
　　So rest your tired old head."

Then Grandfather Sun goes off to his couch,
While she takes her knitting-work out of its pouch
　　And works away so fast.
She watches the children in their cribs,
The boys in trousers and babies in bibs,
　　And then she thinks on the past.

She thinks how different things are now
From the time when first with her tranquil brow
　　She had looked from her seat so high ;
And she wonders whether the babies then,
Who did not grow to be women and men,
　　Had turned to stars in the sky.

She peeps into garrets poor and mean,
Where light and fire are rarely seen,
　　And pities the babies there.
And then she looks at the little boy
Who is smiling in his sleep for joy
　　In his crib of rosewood rare.

THE BOY AND THE FISHES. P 17.

She says, " I am proud of the boys and girls
With rosy cheeks and shining curls,
  And hearts all free from guile ;
But I tenderly love the little ones
Who know not the light of happy homes,
  But bask in my motherly smile."

So Grandmamma Moon her long watch keeps,
While soundly my little darling sleeps
  Tired out with childish play
Till the sun wakes up from his morning nap,
When she quickly dons her own night-cap,
  And we see her no more all day.

THE BOY AND THE FISHES.

THERE once did live a little boy
Who filled his mother's heart with joy;
He said his lessons every day,
And then ran off to romp and play.

2

One day he went to catch some fish,
Carrying a basket and a dish, —
A dish in which some bait he took,
To tempt the fishes in the brook.

His wicker basket held a cake,
Of which he meant his lunch to make;
Besides the nicest of butter and bread,
And the biggest of apples, juicy and red.

Then through the wood his way he took,
And sat down close beside the brook,
Just where the grass and violets grew,
And into the stream his line he threw.

Then listening to the drowsy hum
Of insects playing in the sun
He fell asleep beside the stream,
And there he dreamed the funniest dream.

He thought that hosts of little fishes,
Like those we cook and eat in dishes,
Came floundering out upon the bank,
And played on him the queerest prank.

A dozen seized him by the nose,
While dozens more at limbs and clothes
Pulled hard, until, by hook or crook,
They pulled the boy into the brook.

They sank way down till they had come
To where the king-trout had his home ;
Deep underneath the shining water
The fishes dragged their prisoner after.

At last before the king they stood,
Who, perched upon a log of wood,
Was very pompous, fat, and shining,
In dark brown coat with silver lining.

The fishes sat their captive down
Before the king, who, with a frown
That made the boy in terror shake,
With deep and solemn voice, thus spake :

" O cruel boy, how dare you stand
Before our helpless little band,
And think what mischief you had planned ?

" I wonder how you dare to look
Upon my face here in this brook,
Where you have thrown a jagged hook.

"And is this then your cruel plan,
To catch as many as you can,
Then cook us in a frying-pan?

"How would you like to have a pin
Stuck through your mouth, both out and in,
And then have cook scrape off your skin?"

But here the boy grew very sad,
He did n't think he 'd been so bad;
And so he told the old king trout
If he would only let him out
And send him home to his dear mother,
He 'd never, never catch another.

At this the fish set up a shout,
You never heard such noise from trout, —
So loud, the boy's eyes opened wide,
And there he lay the brook beside.

MOVING INTO THE COUNTRY. P. 21.

Along the path through the green wood
The boy walked home in thoughtful mood,
And never since in pond or brook
Has he been known to throw a hook.

And when they say, "'T was but a dream,
All sights you saw beneath the stream,"
He only says, " Were *I* a fish
To swallow hooks I should n't wish."

MOVING INTO THE COUNTRY.

THE chairs were piled on one another,
  The tables lay, their up side down ;
All things were in a dreadful hubbub,
  For Fred was going out of town.

" Whoa ! " cried the coachman in the doorway,
  Whose horses do not like to wait.
" Pray hurry," calls papa to mamma,
  "I 'm quite afraid we shall be late."

The baby crows to see the bustle,
  Fred dances round for very joy,
And shouts, " Now, all this long, long summer
  I 'm going to be a country boy."

' Whiz! whiz! chee! chee! sounds the steam-engine!
  Now they are safely in the cars.
Fred sees some daisies by the car-track,
  And thinks they look like little stars.

Away they go, — the road looks greener,
  The trees are filled with tender leaves,
And swallows fly with bits of mosses,
  Building their nests beneath the eaves.

And when they reach the nice old farm-house,
  All things seem waiting for their guest;
The lilac-tree wears all its blossoms,
  The crocuses are gayly drest.

Fred runs to count the new-hatched chickens,
  He bids the cow and calf " Good-day!'
And climbing high up in the barn loft,
  He hunts for eggs among the hay.

Where are the rabbits? — Freddy finds them
  And gives them clover leaves to eat;
He sees how proud the peacock marches,
  And laughs at his big ugly feet.

And when the night comes, much too early,
  A tired boy is little Fred ;
He eats his bread and milk for supper,
  And, very sleepy, goes to bed.

THE CHIMNEY SWALLOWS.

THREE little swallows cried "Peep! peep!"
  In their nest in the chimney high ;
They could not see the grass or the trees,   ·
  But only the bright blue sky.

On every side they saw the bricks,
  All dirty and black with smoke,
And they lifted up their heads for joy,
  Whenever the mother-bird spoke.

All day their mother brought to them
  Some worms and seeds of grain;
All day they listened and peeped for her
  As she came and went again.

At night, when the blue sky went away,
  And all was still and dark,
They saw above their heads a star,
  Like a tiny, twinkling spark.

The summer came, and their feathers grew,
  Their wings waxed strong and stout;
Till at length one day their mother said, —
  " 'T is time for my birds to be out."

Then each little bird he fluttered, and tried
  To spread his tender wings;
While the mother flew, to show them how,
  The downy, trembling things.

When all at once, with sudden spring,
  They flew up out of the nest,
And perched all three on the chimney-top,
  Then sat there awhile to rest.

What a new, brave world the swallows saw,
  How they opened wide their eyes;
They did not know the river from sky,
  Or the flowers from butterflies.

They sat and looked for a long, long time,
  They scarcely sang a word;
" Oh, what a beautiful new world,"
  Said the littlest swallow-bird.

I know some little boys and girls,
  Not so happy as birds like these;
For they live 'mid bricks and dirt and smoke,
  And never see the trees.

They do not know how the flowers grow,
  They see but a bit of the sky;
And they hardly see the moon and stars,
  The houses round are so high.

And if they ever grow strong and stout,
  Alas! they have no wings!
To fly above the chimney-tops
  And see God's beautiful things.

Were you sorry for the little birds,
  That lived in the chimney tall?
Then sorry be for the children poor,
  Shut in by the city's wall.

KATYDID.

WHEN the evening star comes out,
  On pleasant summer eves,
You can hear the little Katydids,
  Crying out among the leaves, —
    Katy did, Katy did,
    She did n't, she did n't;
    Katy did, she did,
    No she did n't, Katy did n't.
How I wonder what they mean,
In the leaves, so thick and green,
What the mischief is that's hid,
Which little Katy did?

Was Katy once a little girl,
  Who did n't mind her mother;

Was it only known to Katydids,
  And not to any other?
    Katy did, Katy did,
    She did n't, she did n't ;
    Katy did, she did,
    No she did n't, Katy did n't.
Was she such a naughty girl,
That, through time's unceasing whirl,
These insects are forbid
To tell what Katy did?

My darling on the porch,
  Each eve when they begin,
Tries, with eager little ears,
  To understand their din.
    Katy did, Katy did,
    She did n't, she did n't ;
    Katy did, she did,
    No she did n't, Katy did n't.
But with all their constant cry,
My little one or I
Cannot make out the secret hid,
The dreadful thing that Katy did.

THE BIRDS' SUNDAY.

THE birds were up one Sunday
   With such a chirp and twitter,
You would think for Sabbath morning
   Less noise were surely fitter.

But though the birds may go to church,
   They are not like real people;
And though they heard the ring of bells
   From every spire and steeple,

They did n't mean for all the sound
   To stop their noise and clatter;
So I 'll just tell you what they did,
   And what caused all their chatter.

'T was only that the birds had heard
   A new and famous preacher,
Who rarely came about the place,
   Would this day be their teacher.

So Robin Redbreast and his bride,
  Sweet Jenny Wren, the darling,
Marched off to church, while following fast
  Came swallow, dove, and starling.

And, 'mongst the rest, the gentle thrush,
  Whose notes were thought the sweetest;
With her the modest sparrow walked,
  Whose dress was called the neatest;

Then all the birds, both great and small,
  Hopped, flew, and walked to meeting,
Or stopped upon their way to chat,
  And give their neighbors greeting.

Their church was in a spacious wood;
  The front door was two larches,
And the high ceiling overhead
  Was formed of leafy arches.

The carpet was of tender grass,
  Where little tufts of mosses,
With here and there a tiny flower,
  The vivid green embosses.

The minister was August Rain,
  A very gracious person,
With silver hair, dressed all in gray,—
  Not usual suit of parson.

Yet though his dress was not the thing,
  Indeed, scarce could be meaner,
Where'er he walked with gentle step,
  The grass and flowers grew greener.

His voice was very soft and low;
  The birds must closely listen,
Or they would lose the tender voice
  Which made the flowers glisten.

"My darlings," said the August Rain,
  "I 'm glad to give you greeting,
And glad to see a sober sky
  Can't keep the birds from meeting.

"My lesson for to-day is this:
  'When clouds and skies are grayest,
Sometimes behind the darkest cloud
  The sun shines out the gayest.'"

Much on this text preached August Rain, —
  'T would take too long to say it ;
He gave them heaps of good advice, —
  They promised to obey it.

When, just as he had nearly done,
  The birds burst out in singing,
For down among their church's aisles
  The sun his rays was flinging.

While, changed into a misty form,
  The preacher melted slowly ;
His robe of gray turned gold and blue,
  Till he had vanished wholly.

Still all the birds, no whit dismayed,
  Sang on with louder voices,
While their grand organist, South Wind,
  Played softly in the pauses.

And so the meeting lasted long,
  Till day was spent and over,
Then all the birds flew off, to seek
  Their nests in trees and clover.

THE SPIRIT OF THE POND.

WITHIN a nest of circling hills,
　The little pond lay closely hid;
None knew the place but bird and bee,
　The locust and the katydid,
And every flower that loved the shade,
　Or insect fluttering in the sun,
By these the valley and the pond
　Were known and loved by every one.

The sweet-brier opened there its flowers
　To greet the bee, her noisy guest;
Blue violets bloomed beside the pond,
　White lilies floated on its breast;
The willows drooped their slender arms
　To wet them in its waters blue;
Alders stood close, and tried to hide
　The heaven within from human view.

And where the sun shone brightest down
　The daisy wore her head-dress quaint;

While in the coolest, shadiest spots
    The fern breathed out its perfume faint.
Could you have seen this little vale,
    You would have said 't was very fair,
And wondered whether birds and flowers
    Could e'er be aught but happy there.

Yet on one lovely summer morn,
    When all was bright as bright could be,
The little vale was filled with gloom,
    And sorrowful were bird and bee.
The butterflies shut close their wings,
    Each sad flower bowed its drooping head,
The sweet-brier wept, for on this morn
    Their sister, fair Wild Rose, lay dead.

Her pale pink petals faded lie,
    Just fallen on the dewy grass ;
The breezes blowing through the boughs
    Scatter them idly as they pass.
Poor little Rose ! all day the flowers
    Weep for her death with bitter tears,
Nor stay their grief when evening falls
    And the first silver star appears.

3

But when up in the purple sky
  The yellow moon had slowly climbed,
And from the opened primrose cups
  The evening hymn had softly chimed,
The flow'rets heard a soft, low voice
  No ear had ever heard before, —
'T was like the sound of rippling waves
  Or the soft plash of fairy's oar.

And floating o'er the little pond,
  They saw a figure, clothed in mist,
Uplifted on two glittering wings,
  By radiant moonbeams softly kissed.
" Hush ! " said the Spirit of the Pond,
  " I know your griefs, my darling flowers, —
I know when breezes blow too rude,
  And when ye pine for cooling showers.

" And now I know for whom ye weep,
  A sister flow'ret faded lies.
Do ye not know that every year
  The wild rose and the violet dies?
And every flower that gems the grass
  Or hides its blossoms in the shade,

Must shed its petals on the earth
  And see its tender leaflets fade?

" But I, I know that though the flowers
  Each year must wither on the plain,
They all will bloom more sweet and fresh
  When gentle Spring returns again.
Then do not weep. — Did I repine
  When icy Winter bound me fast?
Ah, no! I slept a patient sleep,
  Believing Spring would come at last."

The spirit shook its quivering wings,
  And all the flowers were drenched with spray;
Ere they could look again, the form
  Had swiftly vanished quite away.
But all were comforted at heart,   ·
  They wept no more their darling rose,
And ere the whip-poor-will commenced
  The vale was locked in deep repose.

BUNNY SQUIRREL.

Bunny Squirrel lived in a hollow tree,
　On the edge of a chestnut wood,
And in his house he stored the nuts
　That served for his winter's food.

When the first frost cracked the chestnut burs,
　The squirrel ran swiftly down,
He looked about with his sharp, round eyes,
　For the nuts so shining and brown;

And when he found the morsel sweet,
　He put them into his jaws,
Then ran away to his little house
　On swift and noiseless paws.

The squirrel's house is snug and warm,
　Of bark the walls are made,
In one corner of his nice bedroom
　His store of nuts is laid.

His floor is carpeted with leaves,
   And there his brother and he
Had planned to spend the winter months
   In feasting and in glee.

So every day he gathered his nuts,
   The thrifty little Bun,
Running swiftly away whenever he heard
   The sound of the sportsman's gun.

One autumn day, as his brother and he,
   At the spreading chestnut's root,
Were searching among the dry, brown leaves
   For the newly fallen fruit,

Swifter than fall of a squirrel's foot
   They heard the horrid sound,
The sportsman fired, and poor little Bun
   Saw his brother lie dead on the ground.

How fast he ran up the chestnut-tree,
   He dropped his nuts in his flight,
And hid away in the thickest boughs,
   Out of the sportsman's sight.

Then back he went to his lonely home,
  And looked at his nutty store,
He grieved to think he never should see
  His squirrel-brother more.

And now, as he lives in his little house,
  And sleeps on his bed of leaves,
Whenever he thinks of his comrade lost
  Poor little Bunny grieves.

His hoarded nuts are not so sweet
  Now his brother is gone,
Nothing in life seems pleasant now,
  Because he is all alone.

So he says next Spring he will take a mate
  To share his lonely nest;
And he thinks of a nice little lady Bun,
  He had always liked the best;

How he'll ask her next year if she will be
  His little squirrel wife,
If she'll share with him his cosy house,
  And brighten his lonely life.

LITTLE CRICKET.

A CRICKET lived under a crack in our hearth,
　As snug as a cricket could be,
With all the little cricks safe in his nest,
　What a merry old cricket was he.
　　　　" Chirp — chirrup,
　　　　Chirrup — chirp,"
Oh, the cricket was full of his glee.

When the sun in the morning shines bright on the
　　floor,
　The cricket keeps close in his house,
And when noontime comes and the weather feels warm,
　The cricket is still as a mouse.
　　　　" Chirp — chirrup,
　　　　Chirrup — chirp."
Oh, the cricket is still as a mouse.

⌐6
But when lamps are all lighted and stories told,
　And the games for the day are o'er,
As we sit by the fire and listen awhile,
　Then blithely he chirps from the floor.

"Come — papa,
Papa — come,"
Till we hear his dear step at the door.

O dear little cricket, to sing such glad songs,
  Our hearth shall protect you alway,
And if Bridget should chase you with brush or with
    broom,
  We quickly will bid her to stay.
      "Chirp — chirrup,
      Chirrup — chirp,"
We never will drive you away.

THE FIRST SNOW.

PERCY looked out of the window,
  The sky was heavy and gray;
"Dear mamma," said he, "it is cloudy,
  Do you think it will snow to-day?
There 's one flake just hit the curbstone,
  I wish it only would snow,
I could try my new sled on the sidewalk
  And wear my new mittens, you know.

" O mamma, do look, here 's another,
   It looks like a star made of down,
Now they 're coming thicker and faster,
  See, the rosebush has got a white crown ;
Now I scarcely can see the houses
   Or the people, over the way,
Hurrah ! for the first snow of winter,
   Hurrah ! it is snowing to-day !

" But, mamma, when I 'm so happy,
   Pray, why do you not look glad ?
You do not smile at the snow-storm,
   Your face looks sober and sad."
Then mamma said : " Come, my darling,
   And sit awhile at my knee,
And I 'll tell you, while I 'm sewing,
   What the first snow says to me.

" It says, ' I look soft and downy,
   As I carpet all the street,
But I 'm cold and hard on the pavements
   To the touch of little bare feet.
And when the poor little children
   See me drop down from the sky,

They wish they had shoes and stockings,
  For they know that the winter is nigh.'

"So mamma sits and thinks of the children,'
  And pities them so, you know,
She cannot laugh with her darling,
  In his joy at the first white snow.
For she knows in the winter evenings,
  When he 's tucked up snug in his bed,
Many a poor little boy in the city
  Has no place to lay his head."

Little Percy sat quiet a moment,
  His heart was too full to speak,
And from under his drooping eyelids
  Two tears rolled down his cheek.
" Dear mamma," he said, very softly,
  " I pity those poor little boys ;
Do you think it would help them any
  If I gave them all my toys?

" And, mamma, if you are willing,
  I 'll give them my fine new sled ;

Perhaps some boy could sell it,
  And buy him a nice little bed.
I did not think of the beggar-boys
  Or their little bare feet at all;
Do you think it was wrong to be happy
  When I saw the snow-flakes fall?"

"Oh, no, it is right to be happy,
  And the dear, good Father in heaven
Is glad when his darling children
  Enjoy the good he has given.
But keep your heart always tender,
  My precious little boy,
And do not forget the wretched,
  When your day is sunny with joy."

THE END.

www.ingramcontent.com/pod-product-compliance
Lightning Source LLC
Chambersburg PA
CBHW021235260626
47172CB00002B/773